The Lost Boys

Hook's Crew

For information regarding permission, write to:
Disney Licensed Publishing, 114 Fifth Avenue, New York, New York 10011

ISBN 0-7172-6660-5

Printed in the U.S.A.   First printing, May 2002

PETER PAN

IN

DISNEY'S

RETURN TO
NEVER·LAND

SCHOLASTIC INC.

New York   Toronto   London   Auckland   Sydney
Mexico City   New Delhi   Hong Kong   Buenos Aires

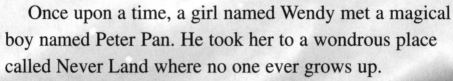

Once upon a time, a girl named Wendy met a magical
boy named Peter Pan. He took her to a wondrous place
called Never Land where no one ever grows up.

When Wendy returned home, she promised,
"I'll always believe in you, Peter Pan."

Years passed. Wendy grew up, but she never forgot her promise. Every night, Wendy told her two children stories about Peter Pan, the Lost Boys, and a tiny fairy named Tinker Bell.

Wendy's daughter, a serious twelve-year-old named Jane, had no use for make-believe. But her brother, Danny, loved hearing the stories again and again—especially the one about Captain Hook and the treasure . . .

Captain Hook and his men stole treasure from other ships. They kept their loot on their ship, the *Jolly Roger.*

One night, Peter Pan and the Lost Boys slipped aboard the *Jolly Roger* and stole Hook's treasure. It was all just a great game for Peter.

Peter and Hook had a long, fierce sword fight. Eventually, Peter and the boys escaped with the treasure. Then Tinker Bell showered the pirate ship with pixie dust, which made the *Jolly Roger* float off into the sky.

"You've not seen the end of me, Peter Pan. I'll get you for this if it's the last thing I do!" Captain Hook shouted as he drifted away.

"Hook will never
win, as long as there is
faith, trust, and pixie dust," Wendy said
as she ended her story for the night.

Danny was delighted, but not Jane. She thought it
was all just childish nonsense. "Peter Pan isn't real,
and people don't fly."

"They do, too!" cried Danny.

"Oh, Daniel, grow up!" Jane
said and went to her room.

Jane lay
down on a
seat next to
the window.
After a while,
she fell asleep.

While she
slept, something
strange happened in
the sky outside—a
surprise visitor appeared.
It was someone she never, ever expected to see . . .

Jane awoke to see Captain Hook standing next to her!

"Hello, Wendy," Hook said wickedly, thinking Jane was her mother.

Before Jane could explain, Captain Hook ordered his first mate, Mr. Smee, to put her into a big sack.

"My apologies, Miss," Smee said as he tied the sack.

Hook and Smee took Jane aboard the *Jolly Roger* and headed back to Never Land. Hook had a plan to trap Peter Pan once and for all.

"With Wendy as bait, we shall lure Peter Pan to his doom," Hook bragged to Smee.

As luck would have it, just as the pirate ship arrived in Never Land, Peter Pan and Tinker Bell appeared.

Hook's men fired a cannonball at Peter. Of course, they missed.

So Hook pointed to the hanging sack. He boasted that he had captured Wendy and planned to feed her to the Octopus that lurked in the water below.

"Let her go, you black-hearted scoundrel!"
commanded Peter as he and Hook began a sword fight.
    "You want her? Ha! Well go and get her!"
Hook shouted.

Captain Hook raised his sword and cut the rope holding the sack.

To Peter's horror, the sack dropped into the water.

Bravely, Peter dived into the water to save his friend. Tinker Bell followed close behind— Peter might need her help.

Captain Hook and the pirates peered
eagerly over the side of the ship. After a short
while, Peter's hat bobbed up to the surface.

Minutes later, when Peter didn't appear,
Captain Hook shouted triumphantly, "I did it!
I did it! I'm free—free of Peter Pan forever!"

But Hook's cheering was cut short. Out of the water rose Peter Pan and Tinker Bell! Peter flew away with the sack in his arms.

Tinker Bell sprinkled pixie dust onto the giant Octopus, causing it to rise high above the *Jolly Roger*.

Then Tinker Bell abruptly stopped sprinkling pixie dust. The Octopus landed on top of Captain Hook with a loud *CRASH!*

Hook yowled as the beast started to pull him over the side of the ship.

The hungry Octopus was very happy to
have caught a Captain-Hook dinner! But the
captain wasn't so happy about *being* dinner.
    "Smeeee!" Hook yelled.

Smee grabbed Captain
Hook's hand. Smee and the
Octopus pulled and pulled
in opposite directions.

Finally, with a mighty yank, Smee wrenched the captain out of the Octopus's arms. The two pirates flew through the air and fell into the cargo hold.

Smee had saved Hook. But the captain wasn't the least bit grateful.

"Mr. Smee, be a good fellow and fix the plank, please," Hook growled. "So I can make you walk it!"

Meanwhile, Peter
and Tinker Bell flew
to safety.

Peter gently placed
the sack on the ground
and began to untie it.
He couldn't wait to see
his old friend, Wendy!

But when Peter opened
the sack . . . *Pow!*

Thinking she was still
a prisoner of the pirates,
Jane had let loose a
terrific punch.

"Ow! You're sure not Wendy!" Peter said rubbing
his jaw.

Just then Hook fired a cannonball at them.
Peter flew off with Jane in his arms.

"If you're not Wendy, who are you?" Peter asked.

"I'm her
daughter—Jane,"
the girl replied.

As they flew over Never Land, Jane
was amazed at all the sights below her.
Suddenly Peter stopped flying and
dropped Jane into a hollow tree trunk.
She slid down a very long chute.

Jane landed at the bottom of the underground tree house where Peter lived with the Lost Boys.

Nibs, Slightly, the Twins, Cubby, and Tootles dropped down from the ceiling to greet her.

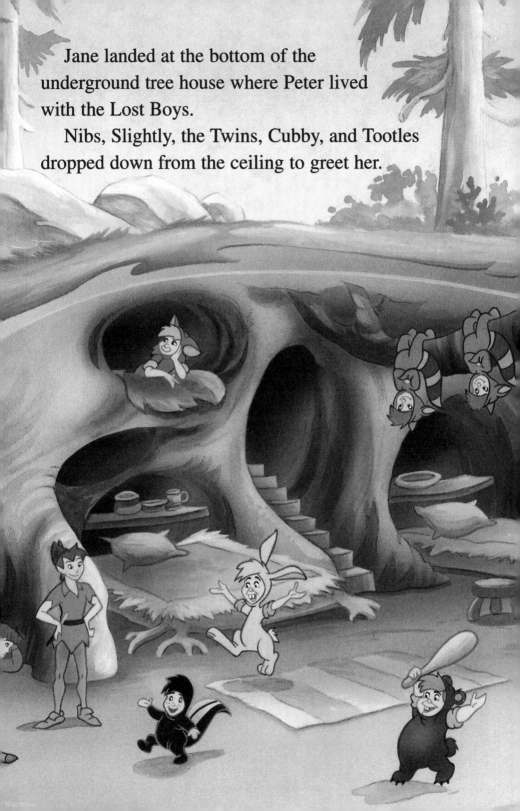

"This is Jane!" Peter told the boys. "She's gonna stay here and be our new mother and tell us stories!"

The Lost Boys gathered around Jane excitedly.

But Tinker Bell wasn't so pleased. She wanted Jane to go home. Tinker Bell didn't want to share Peter Pan's attention.

"Let's play a game!"
said Nibs.

"How about Treasure
Hunt?" Peter suggested.

But Jane didn't want
to play.

"No, no, no, no, no, no!"
Jane shouted.

"I have to go home," Jane told them and stomped off.

"What's the matter with her?" asked Cubby.

Peter scratched his chin and thought hard.

"I don't know," he said. "She acts kinda like a grown-up."

"Ewww!" said the Lost Boys.

Peter followed Jane and soon found her building a raft so that she could sail home.

He watched as Jane pushed her raft into the water and jumped on board.

But she didn't get far!

Almost immediately, the raft began to break
up and sink.

Jane fell into the water with a big *SPLASH!*

When he saw she was in trouble, Peter flew
out to save Jane.

"The only way out of here is to fly," Peter explained. Then he set her down on top of a ledge.

"Anybody can do it," Peter assured her. All it took was faith, trust, and pixie dust.

But Jane refused to believe she could fly.
So Tinker Bell sprinkled some pixie dust on
the Lost Boys, and they glided in the air
around her to show her how it worked.

Then Peter asked
Tinker Bell to sprinkle
Jane with pixie dust, too.
But Tinker Bell didn't want
to do anything to help Jane!
She thought that Peter liked
Jane too much.

Peter knew just
how to persuade
Tinker Bell. "Gosh,
if Jane can't fly
home, I guess she'll
have to move in with
us," he whispered to
the tiny fairy.

Tinker Bell didn't like that idea at all! So she
sprinkled Jane with lots and lots of pixie dust.
But all the dust just made
Jane sneeze.

Now Peter was *sure* that Jane could fly. So he nudged her off the ledge. But Jane didn't have the faith and trust she needed to fly.

"Ahhhh!!!" Jane cried as she fell. The Lost Boys tried to catch her, but they missed. Jane landed in the soft ground with a *THUD*.

Jane was terribly angry and upset. "Leave me alone!" she cried. "I don't believe in any of this—and I especially don't believe in fairies!"

As Jane stormed away, Tinker Bell began falling towards the ground. She could no longer fly, and her light was fading.

Peter knelt down to hear what Tinker
Bell was saying.
A worried Peter told the Lost Boys,
"If we don't get Jane to believe in fairies,
Tink's light is gonna go out!"
The group sped off to find Jane.

Meanwhile, Jane came upon Captain Hook, who was weeping miserably. He told her that Peter Pan had stolen his treasure. But Hook needed it to sail home to his mother!

Captain Hook promised to take Jane home if she helped him find the treasure. Jane agreed, and he gave her a whistle to signal him when she found the treasure.

Jane didn't know it, but she had been tricked into Captain Hook's plan to capture Peter Pan!

Soon Jane met up with Peter and the Lost Boys. "Jane, I'm awful sorry," Peter said. "We want to do something to make it up to ya. We want you to feel like you're one of us."

"Well," Jane said, "why don't we play . . . Treasure Hunt?"

"That's a great idea!" said Peter. "But you'll have to *think* like a Lost Boy and have *fun* like a Lost Boy."

Jane couldn't
remember the last time
she'd had so much fun!
Eventually, Jane discovered the treasure.

Then she remembered Hook's whistle. Jane realized
that she didn't want to betray her new friends, so she
threw the whistle away.

Unfortunately,
Tootles saw the
shiny whistle,
picked it up, and
blew it loudly!

"No, wait! No!"
Jane cried out.
But it was too late!

Captain Hook and the pirates heard the whistle and in no time captured Peter and the Lost Boys.

Hook thanked Jane. "I couldn't have done it without you!" he told her.

"You're a traitor, Jane!" Peter shouted angrily. "And because you don't believe in fairies, Tink's light is going out!"

Hook took Peter and the Lost Boys back to his ship. This time, he wasn't going to let Peter get away!

Jane needed Tinker Bell's help, but she found the tiny fairy very weak.

Jane started to cry. "I'm so sorry!" she said, because she *did* believe in fairies.

Then something magical happened! Tinker Bell's light started to flicker. Soon the fairy's light was shining brighter than ever before!

Jane and Tinker Bell arrived at the *Jolly Roger*
just in the nick of time. They easily outwitted
Hook, especially when Tinker Bell sprinkled Jane
with pixie dust and Jane *flew* away before Hook
could capture her.

Then, just after Jane freed Peter, Hook made
another attempt to grab her.

"Gotcha!" Hook bellowed as he swung on a
rope towards her.

But Peter swiftly grabbed his dagger and cut the
rope. Hook fell into the water . . .

. . . and onto the Octopus!

"Smeeee!" yelled Hook as he tried to escape.

"Let's hear it for Jane—the one and only Lost Girl!" the Lost Boys shouted.

Peter looked sad. "You can fly now. You can go home," he told Jane.

"I'll miss you," Jane admitted. "But now I have great stories to tell . . . all about Peter Pan and the Lost Boys!"

So Peter Pan, Tinker Bell, and Jane flew back to Jane's home in London.

At home, Jane and her family were
very happy to be reunited!

Jane told her mother and Danny about
her adventures in Never Land—about
pirates and treasure, the giant Octopus,
Tinker Bell, and especially Peter Pan.

Peter saw that his old friend Wendy was now
a grown-up.

"You've changed," he told her.

"Not really. Not ever," Wendy answered.

Wendy would always believe in Peter Pan—
and now Jane would, too.